To Grace, for her encouragement and support

I LIKE TO READ is a registered trademark of Holiday House, Inc.

Copyright © 2015 by Pat Schories
All Rights Reserved
HOLIDAY HOUSE is registered in the U.S. Patent and Trademark Office.
Printed and Bound in April 2015 at Tien Wah Press, Johor Bahru, Johor, Malaysia.
The artwork was created with traditional watercolors on cold press watercolor paper.
www.holidayhouse.com
First Edition
1 3 5 7 9 10 8 6 4 2

Library of Congress Cataloging-in-Publication Data
Schories, Pat, author, illustrator.
Pie for Chuck / Pat Schories. — First edition.
pages cm. — (I like to read)
Summary: "Chuck and his woodland friends desperately want a taste of freshly-baked pie,
but they can't get it down from the windowsill"— Provided by publisher.
ISBN 978-0-8234-3392-6 (hardcover)
[1. Forest animals—Fiction. 2. Pies—Fiction.] I. Title.
PZ7.S37645Pie 2015
[E]—dc23
2014039823

ISBN 978-0-8234-3423-7 (paperback)

Pie for Chuck

by **Pat Schories**

I Like to Read®

Holiday House / New York

Big Chuck loves pie.

Big Chuck can
see the pie.

Big Chuck can smell the pie.

Big Chuck cannot get the pie.

Can Raccoon get the pie?

No, he cannot!

Can Rabbit get the pie?

No, he cannot!

Can Chip get the pie?

No, he cannot!

Can the mice get the pie?

No, they cannot!

Can the mice get the pie now?

Yes, they can!

Pie for Chuck.

Pie for everyone!

Have You Eaten?

A Story of Food, Friendship, and Kindness

Su Youn Lee

FEIWEL AND FRIENDS • NEW YORK

Coco loved sweet potatoes,

and she loved to share them

with everyone around her.

She often asked the question, "Have you eaten?"
Her neighbors thought it was odd, but they didn't
mind, because Coco was sweet like sweet potatoes.

Every morning, Coco attended a painting class.
One day, she noticed a new student,
Caroline, sitting alone.

"How's your painting going?" Coco asked.
"Not well. I'm out of white ink, but I don't
know who to ask for more."

"Why don't you use mine?"
Coco asked. "Have you eaten?"

Coco offered Caroline a sweet potato. As they
ate together, Caroline no longer felt lonely. She
felt like she had found a friend.

After painting class, Coco headed to the library.
She noticed the twins Ping and Pong stacking books
while their mother, Popo, tried to get them to read.

"Hello, twins. What are you doing?" asked Coco.

"We're building a fort!" they replied. "But the books keep falling!"

"Well, building a book fort is a lot of work. Have you eaten?"

Coco offered Popo and the twins sweet potatoes.
As they ate together, Ping and Pong no longer
felt tired. They felt like they could build anything.

In the evening, Coco exercised in the park.
She noticed Pocky crying on a bench.
"What's wrong, Pocky?" asked Coco.

"I struck out again," sniffed Pocky. "I think our baseball team lost because of me."

"It's okay to feel bad, but you'll get another chance. Have you eaten?"

"I'm not in the mood to eat," said Pocky.

No thanks!

RUMBLE~

Coco reached into her bag and pulled out two sweet potatoes.

Coco offered Pocky a sweet potato.

As they ate together, Pocky no longer felt sad.

He felt like he could try again.

The next day, Caroline went to painting class. She wanted to thank Coco for keeping her company, but Coco wasn't there.

Popo, Ping, and Pong searched for Coco at the library. They wanted to read a book with Coco, but she wasn't there, either.

Pocky ran around the park. He wanted to tell Coco that his team had won, but he couldn't find her anywhere.
Where was Coco?

Coco was in bed, sick. She felt lonely, tired, and sad.

Just as Coco was about to fall asleep,
she heard the doorbell ring.
"Who could that be?" Coco wondered.

It was Caroline, Popo, Ping, Pong, and Pocky.
"Oh, Coco. Have you eaten?" they asked.

Caroline brought a lemon to make lemonade.
Popo and the twins brought ingredients to make chicken
soup. And Pocky brought ice to bring down Coco's fever.

As Coco watched her new friends cook, she no longer felt lonely, tired, and sad. They were happy to share their food, and Coco was happy to have them as friends.

Coco's friends finally understood why Coco asked her
question, and soon it became their favorite question, too.

AUTHOR'S NOTE

"Have you eaten?" "식사 하셨어요?" (formal) or "밥 먹었어?" (informal)
Shik-sa ha shuh ssuh yo? / Bap muh guh ssuh?

In Korea, we often greet family, friends, or even people we've just met by asking, "Have you eaten?"

It's not simply asking if someone ate a meal.

It's the same as asking, "How are you?"

While sharing food and eating together are important parts of Korean culture, the phrase, "Have you eaten?" became widely used as a greeting after World War II and the Korean War. Korea was one of the poorest countries in the world and many people didn't have enough to eat.

To show concern about another person, Koreans would ask, "Have you eaten?"

Food is much more abundant today, but the phrase continues to be used as a greeting to show that you care about a person.

So if your Korean friend asks, "Have you eaten?" it means they care about you.

Coco's Cooking Class

Hannah Yam  Garnet/Jewel  Asian/Japanese  Murasaki

Before you start cooking, you will need 3-4 Japanese sweet potatoes.
If you can't find the right ones, Murasaki sweet potatoes are another good option.

1 Wash the sweet potatoes.

2 Place them on an oven tray.

3 Preheat your oven to 350 degrees for 10-15 minutes and place the sweet potatoes on a rack in the middle.

4 Use a chopstick to poke the middle of a potato. If the chopstick goes through easily, then it's ready to eat.

5 The sweet potatoes are much tastier if you let them rest on the tray with the oven door closed for 30 minutes.

6 Enjoy!

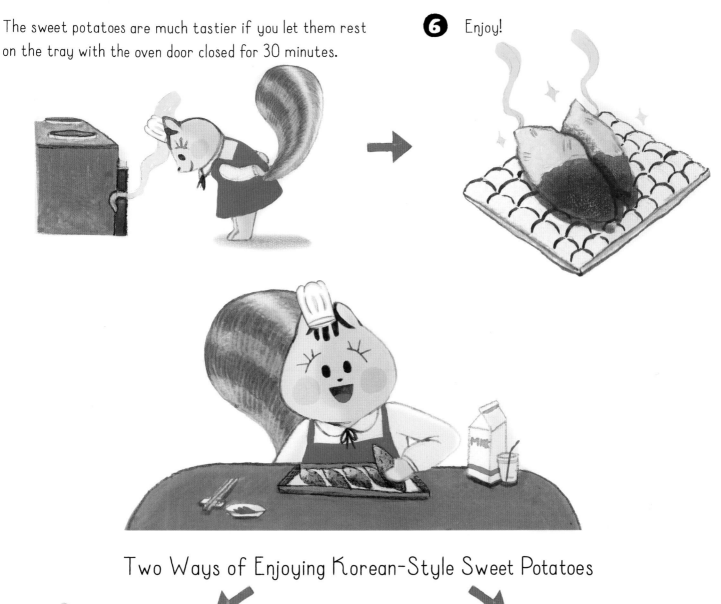

Two Ways of Enjoying Korean-Style Sweet Potatoes

The traditional Korean way of enjoying baked sweet potatoes is with kimchi, adding a piece of kimchi on the sweet potato before taking each bite.

If you're not familiar with kimchi, baked sweet potatoes are always good with milk.

To J.C., Haon, and the many Cocos
who took care of me with love

get
1 BOX of
sweetpotatoes

sweet
potatoes K

A FEIWEL AND FRIENDS BOOK

An imprint of Macmillan Publishing Group, LLC

120 Broadway, New York, NY 10271

mackids.com

Our books may be purchased in bulk for promotional, educational, or

business use. Please contact your local bookseller or the Macmillan

Corporate and Premium Sales Department at (800) 221-7945

ext. 5442 or by email at MacmillanSpecialMarkets@macmillan.com.

Library of Congress Cataloging-in-Publication Data is available.

First edition, 2022

Book design by Aram Kim

Mixed medium

Feiwel and Friends logo designed by Filomena Tuosto

Printed in China by RR Donnelley Asia Printing Solutions Ltd.,

Dongguan City, Guangdong Province

ISBN 978-1-250-79114-6 (hardcover)

1 3 5 7 9 10 8 6 4 2